Bob the BOOGER Fairy

Written by Robert S. Nott · Illustrated by Lara Ede

make
believe
ideas

Fairyland was a place where **all fairies** could follow their dreams and find **fame** and **fortune**.
But **not** every fairy was famous.

And in a far, forgotten corner of Fairyland,
beyond the magic dust and wands,
lived one of those fairies.

His name was **Bob.**

FAIRY AVENUE

FLUTTER STREET

MAGIC DUST DRIVE

SPARKLE BOULEVARD

BOOGER CANYON

SNOTTY HILLS

Bob →

Bob was the BOOGER Fairy.

It was his job to dispose of the things from your nose!

Bob was the number-one **booGer** expert in all of Fairyland.

He knew the **difference** between a **Thin 'n' Flaky** and an **Icky-Sticky-Flicky.** Or a **Cluster Chunk** and a **Nose-Snorter.**

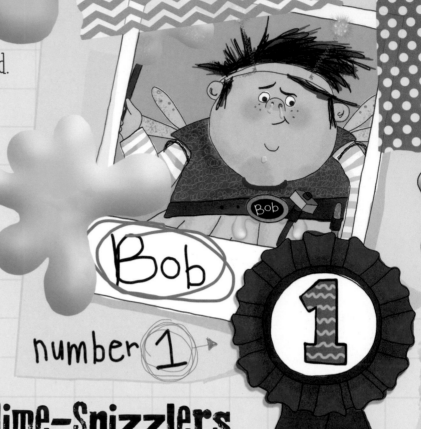

Bob

number 1

He even knew how to deal with a bad case of **Slime-Snizzlers.**

THIN 'N' FLAKY

a super-thin dried nasal mucus that is almost see-through, perfect for fairy-house glazing.

tooth fairy windows

ICKY-STICKY-FLICKY

one of those annoying boogers that no matter how many times you flick...it won't disappear!

Morning Pick	Showbiz Smear	Snot Spa	Slime Porridge	Nose Forest	Booger Breath

CLUSTER CHUNK

a collection of different-colored boogers that have been squeezed and squashed together over a very long time!

NOSE-SNORTER

a booger that is easy to locate but super hard to scoop out.

SLIME-SNIZZLER

a half-booger, half-slimy-snot that clings like **gloopy** string to the <u>inside</u> of your <u>nose.</u>

However, being good at his job **wasn't** enough for Bob...

"I don't think you'd make a very good Fairy Godmother."

"We've decided to go with Tony the Toenail Fairy … he's got his own scissors."

Then, one day, Bob's luck changed.
While he chiseled, scraped, and mined
down the side of **snotty** Simon's bed
(Simon was a secret smearer)...

...something gleamed and glistened among the
Cluster Chunks and the **Icky-Sticky-Flickies.**

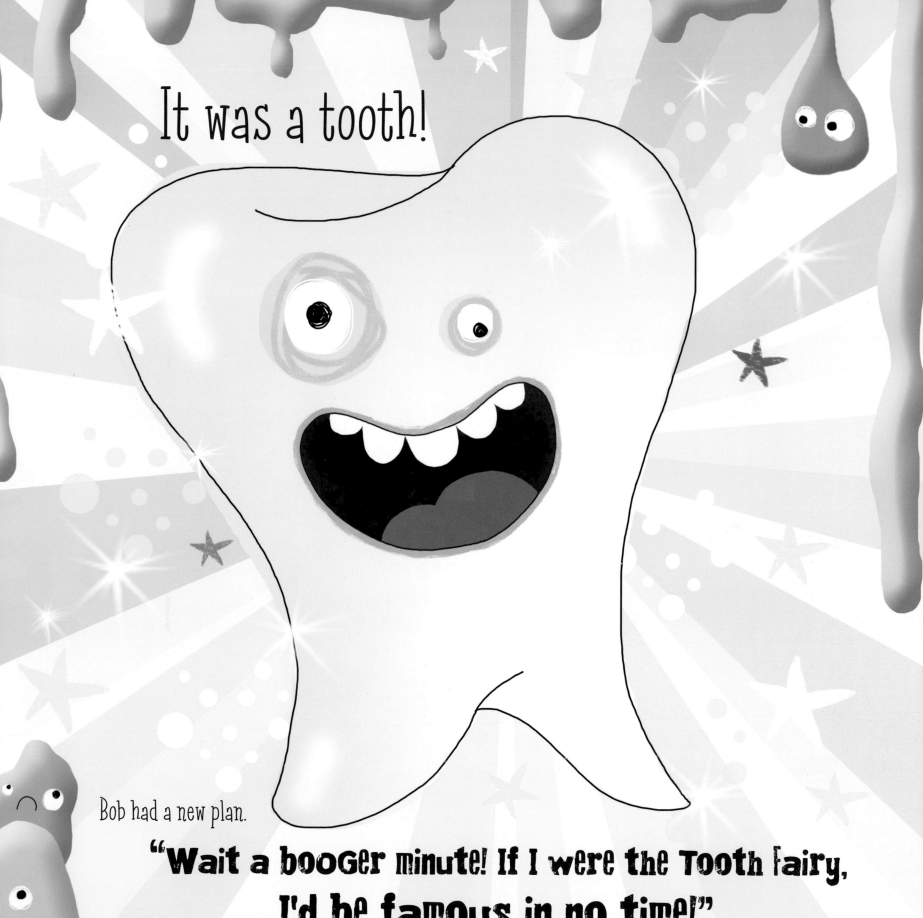

So Bob built a **booger** trap, tucked Simon's tooth under his pillow, and waited silently, until the Tooth Fairy appeared.

Bob burst from the bed... and **flopped** into his own **booger** trap!
The Tooth Fairy smiled — she knew exactly what Bob wanted.

"Hmmm, I could do with a rest," she said.
"Do you mind being the Tooth Fairy
for a while?"

Bob didn't hesitate:
**"Absolutely!
I won't let you down."**

Bob started his Tooth Fairy duties right away.

He flew from pillow to pillow, collecting tooth after tooth.

"This isn't that hard.

I'm going to be the best, most famous Tooth Fairy ever!" said Bob.

However, as morning dawned, the toothless children were in for a **shock.**

For under their pillows, instead of a **shiny tooth-fairy coin . . .**

Bob thought he had done a brilliant job, so you can imagine his reaction when he saw the **Fairyland Star's** front page.

FAIRYLAND STAR

WHAT'S HAPPENED TO THE TOOTH FAIRY?

BOOGERS DISCOVERED... UNDER PILLOWS

WHO IS THE BOOGER-MAN?

He was finally in the news ... but for all the **wrong** reasons!

Bob fluttered home. His dreams of **fame** and **fortune** had turned into a nightmare.

The **Tooth Fairy** tried to make Bob feel better: "Being famous isn't all it's cracked up to be," she told him. "It's what we do that matters."

"Imagine the mess if the Toenail Fairy didn't clean up everyone's nail clippings.

Or if the Fart Fairy wasn't around to vacuum up all those stinky smells.

And imagine what would happen if you didn't collect all those unwanted boogers. It would be a..."

...and with no one to dispose of the things from your nose,
the **booger** mess had grown bigger...and bigger...and BIGGER!

"It looks like you have an important job to do!" said the Tooth Fairy.

"YOU'RE right! The world needs the BOOGER fairy!" declared Bob.

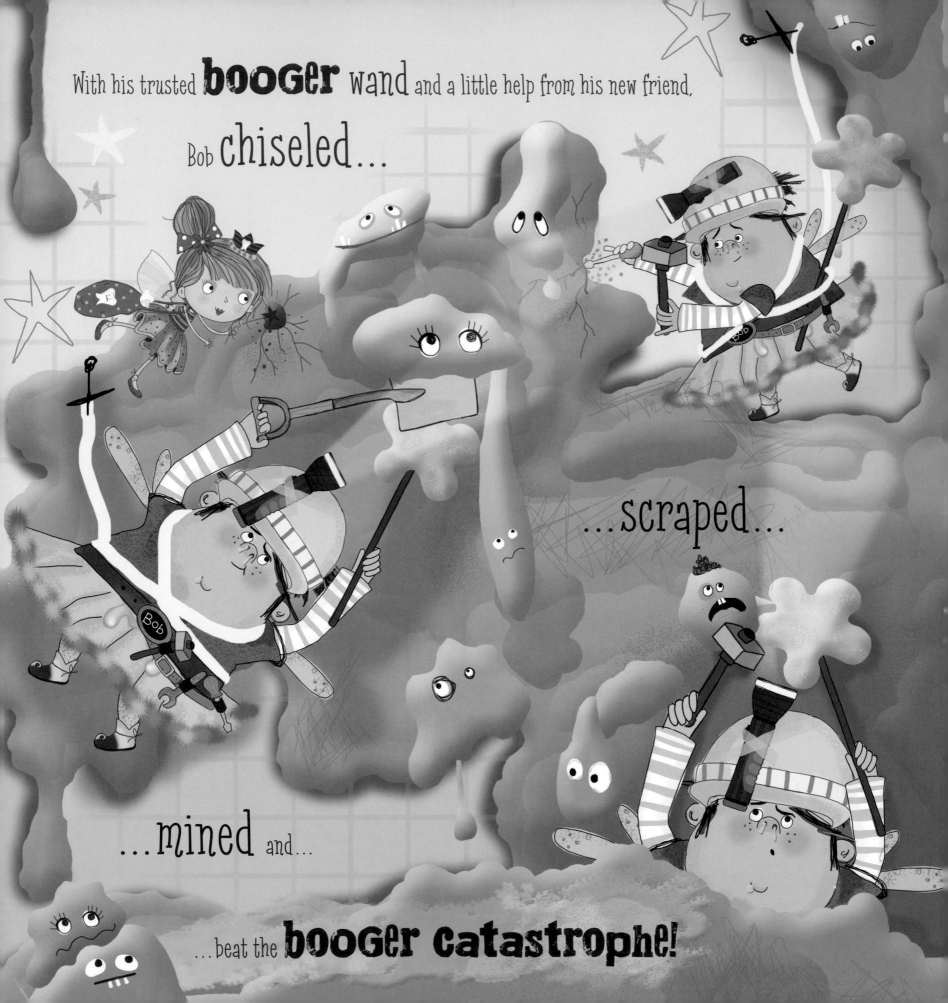

Everyone gathered for an interview with the **fairy-of-the-moment**.
"Where's Bob the **SUPER-BOOGER** Fairy?" But Bob had fluttered back to Fairyland.

Although Bob wanted to be famous more than anything else, he realized he didn't want to be famous for being the fairy that had made the **booger catastrophe** — even if he had saved the day!

Bob now knew he wanted to be famous for doing something **good**.
So with an **epic fairy tale** worth telling...he wrote **this** book!

"I'm FAMOUS!"

(And I hope you'll agree — his story was **booger-brilliant!**)

THE END